PUGBY THE PUG
DISCOVERS RUGBY

**ILLUSTRATED BY
CHAD THOMPSON**

**WRITTEN BY
AARON HOWES**

This book is dedicated to my wife SARAH, I love you very much and wouldn't have been able to do this without you. My boys FINN and CAYDEN, I hope you find something that you enjoy as much as I do rugby. And CAPTAIN POWER for getting me started on the pug journey.

One day, PUGBY THE PUG decided he was going to find a **sport to play.**

He had heard from his friends that sports were

oodles and zoodles of fun.

Since there are so many sports in our wide, wide world, he knew this would be

quite an adventure.

So he ate a healthy breakfast and went out to start learning.

The first thing PUGBY found was a group of friends **running** races.

But PUGBY THE PUG didn't have the

longest legs, or the quickest paws.

He had trouble keeping up.

PUGBY decided that was perfectly okie dokie, and he would keep on looking.

Later that day, PUGBY
saw some friends doing
high jumping.

But PUGBY THE PUG didn't have the

springiest legs, or the

strongest knees.

He had trouble
jumping over
the bar.

PUGBY decided that was

perfectly okie dokie,

and he would keep on looking.

Finally, PUGBY saw some friends **swimming** races.

But PUGBY THE PUG didn't have the **strongest arms,** or a **belly that floated very well.**

He had trouble moving through the water.

PUGBY decided that was perfectly okie dokie,

and he would keep on looking.

Just when

PUGBY THE PUG

was worried he might never

**find a Sport that
matched him best,**

he saw animals of all

Shapes and Sizes

in a field.

They were playing with a
big white ball.

"Hi there! Would you like to play with us?"

Marshall the Moose asked.

PUGBY explained that he was worried that he wouldn't be

fast enough,

jumpy enough,

or **Strong enough** to play.

"**Nonsense!** This sport has something for **everyone!**"
Hailey the Hippo said.

"**I'm the strong one** who **lifts** people up and **keeps people safe** in the silly sounding scrum."

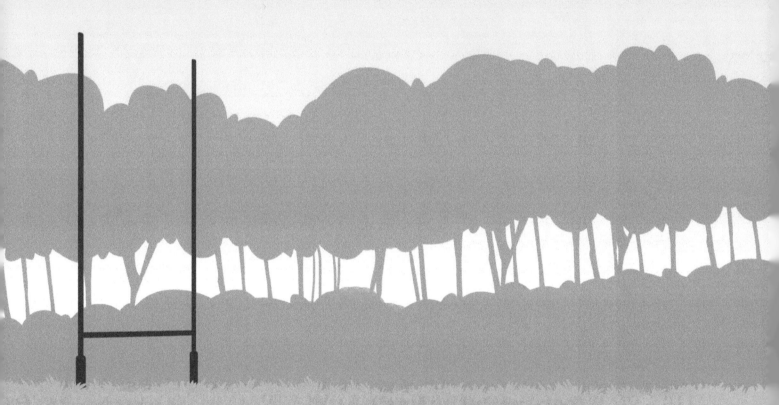

"And I'm the tall one,"
Marshall the Moose said,

"I **catch** the ball at the
tippy tippy top of the line and
stretch my **looooong looooong**
legs to try and block kicks."

"And I'm the quick one,"
Rhylie the Roadrunner said.

"I run down the field with the ball so fast that I look like a lightning bolt that goes BAZIIIINNG!!"

"But what can I do?"
PUGBY asked.

"Everyone has something they can do in this game!!"

Rhylie excitedly replied.

"We just have to work together to discover what you like to do. Then we can put all our skills together to make a great team!"

PUGBY tried out some of the many fun things you can do in this sport. He found that he really liked

throwing and **catching**

the **big white ball,** and his aim was pretty good!

"The most important thing is to have **fun, fun, fun!**" Marshall said. "You don't have to run the **fastest**, jump the **highest**, or be the **strongest**. We all **work together** to play this game, and we have a home for all different kinds of animals."

PUGBY also really liked the idea of **having fun, fun, fun all day,** and **being part of a team.**

"What do you call this game?"

an excited PUGBY asked.

all the animals cheered together.

RUGBY!

PUGBY and **Rugby**,

what a perfect match!

PUGBY THE PUG
knew he'd found his

perfect sport,

and that was

super duper okie dokie.

 FriesenPress

One Printers Way
Altona, MB R0G 0B0
Canada

www.friesenpress.com

Illustrated by Chad Thompson

ISBN
978-1-03-912373-1 (Hardcover)
978-1-03-912372-4 (Paperback)
978-1-03-912374-8 (eBook)

1. JUVENILE FICTION, SPORTS & RECREATION, GAMES

Distributed to the trade by The Ingram Book Company

Lightning Source UK Ltd.
Milton Keynes UK
UKHW050727220422
401857UK00005B/233